P9-DEL-578

DATE			

ANNA GROSSNICKLE HINES

Maybe a Band-Aid Will Help

E. P. DUTTON · NEW YORK

for my own Sarah and her Abigail

Copyright © 1984 by Anna Grossnickle Hines

LIBRARY OF CONGRESS CATALOGING IN PUBLICATION DATA

Hines, Anna Grossnickle.
Maybe a Band-Aid will help.
Summary: Trying to get Mama to fix a broken doll takes
a lot of persistence.
[1.Dolls—Fiction]   I. Title.
PZ7.H572May 1984   [E]   84-1533
ISBN 0-525-44115-8

Published in the United States by E. P. Dutton, Inc.,
2 Park Avenue, New York, N.Y. 10016

Published simultaneously in Canada by
Fitzhenry & Whiteside Limited, Toronto

Editor: Ann Durell   Designer: Riki Levinson

Printed in Hong Kong by South China Printing Co.
First Edition   W   10 9 8 7 6 5 4 3 2 1

We were just playing train when
Abigail's leg came off.

"Mama!" I yelled. "Abigail's hurt. Can you fix her?"

"Yes, Sarah," Mama said. "I can sew her leg back on, but not now. First I have to finish making this rocking horse for the craft fair."

Mandy and Ben helped me put Abigail in
the sewing basket. Then they went home.

I had a tuna fish sandwich for lunch. Tuna fish is Abigail's favorite.

Mama still hadn't finished the rocking horse.

I took Hopkins to bed with me for a nap.
His whiskers prickle.

When I got up from my nap, Abigail was
still in the sewing basket.

"Mama, can you fix Abigail now?" I asked.

"Not right now," she said. "I've finished

the horse, but I have to do the laundry so
you'll have clean clothes to wear tomorrow."

"I'll wear dirty ones," I said, but Mama
just shook her head.

I played school with Hopkins and Miss
Mousie. We made pictures for Abigail, and
we wrote, "I hope your leg is better soon."

I took Miss Mousie to bed with me. She
is very soft, and she doesn't have prickly
whiskers. But she takes up too much room.

In the morning I said, "Today! You have
to fix Abigail today, Mama."

"I have to clean the house first," Mama
said. "Then we'll see."

Mandy and Ben came over. Mandy wanted
to play train again. Ben wanted to play school.
I didn't want to play anything without
Abigail.

Then I had an idea.

"We can help my mother, so she'll have time
to fix Abigail. We'll mop the floor for her."

"What are you DOING?" Mama cried.

She made Mandy and Ben go home.

I took Abigail out of the sewing basket.
She was lonely in there. She wanted to go
in my room with me.

"Maybe a Band-Aid will help," I said.
It didn't.

I got Mama's sewing basket.
"I'm going to fix you myself, Abigail.
You'll have to be brave."
Abigail was very brave.

I stuck my finger. I tried to be brave,
too.

Mama heard me.

"I'm sorry," she said. "I didn't mean to
get angry. I know you were trying to help."

She put one of Abigail's Band-Aids on my finger.
"Let's play a game with Abigail," she said.
"What shall it be?"

"Hospital!" I said. "Let's play hospital!"

So I took Abigail to the hospital, and
Dr. Mama fixed her leg as good as new.

Tomorrow Abigail and I might play
hospital with Mandy and Ben.